Judy Moody

and the

NOT Bummer Summer

The Poop Picnic

Judy Moody

and the
NOT BUMMER SUMMER

The Poop Picnic

written by **Jamie Michalak**

Based on the motion picture screenplay
by Megan McDonald and Kathy Waugh

Based on the Judy Moody series by Megan McDonald

CANDLEWICK PRESS

Text copyright © 2011 by Candlewick Press, Inc.
Illustrations copyright © 2011 by CBM Productions, LLC
Judy Moody font copyright © 2003 by Peter H. Reynolds

Based on the theatrical motion picture *Judy Moody and the NOT Bummer Summer,*
produced by Smokewood Entertainment

Judy Moody®. Judy Moody is a registered trademark of Candlewick Press, Inc.

First edition 2011

ISBN 978-0-7636-5553-2

11 12 13 14 15 16 WOR 10 9 8 7 6 5 4 3 2 1

Printed in Stevens Point, WI, U.S.A.

This book was typeset in ITC Cheltamham and Judy Moody.

Candlewick Press
99 Dover Street
Somerville, Massachusetts 02144

visit us at www.candlewick.com
www.judymoodythemovie.com

Contents

CHAPTER ONE

The "I Ate Something Gross" Club

Judy Moody was in a mood. A bummer summer mood.

She found out that her two best friends were going away for the summer.

ROAR!

She found out that her Mom and Dad were going away for the summer, too.

DOUBLE ROAR!

And guess who was coming to stay with Judy and her brother, Stink? Aunt Opal. Also known as Aunt Awful.

Before she went to bed, Judy asked her Magic 8 Ball, "Could this summer get any worse?"

WITHOUT A DOUBT, it said.

Perfect. Judy groaned.

"You sure are in a mood," said Stink.

"You would be, too," said Judy, "if your summer was a total bummer."

But Stink had BIG plans for the summer. BigFOOT plans.

"I'm gonna catch Bigfoot," Stink said. "You can help!"

"Yeah, right," said Judy. "I'd rather catch poison ivy."

"But there are Bigfoot sightings all over town!" Stink said. "My friends from Bigfoot club even saw him at the mall!"

"The only big feet around here are your super-smelly ones!" said Judy.

This, WITHOUT A DOUBT, is going to be the worst summer ever, Judy thought.

But when Aunt Opal arrived, she wasn't awful after all. She brought a huge trunk filled with neat-o art supplies. She wore blue boots and lots of bracelets AND she did yoga on the lawn.

They even got to have tuna-fish pizza for dinner. Rare!

"I hope you saved room for dessert," said Aunt Opal.

She brought out a plate of hot-dog pieces and a bowl of bubbly orange goo.

"What IS that?" asked Judy.

"It looks like Bigfoot barf," Stink said.

Aunt Opal took a piece of hot dog and dipped it in the goo.

"It's called tangerine fondue," she said, and popped it into her mouth. "Mmmm," she said. "Dig in, guys!"

Judy looked at Stink.

Stink looked at Judy.

"You first," Judy said to Stink.

"You think *this* is gross?" said Aunt

Opal. "One time I ate cockroaches."

"You ate bugs?" Judy couldn't

believe her ears. "Gross! Gag me with

a spoon!"

"Tell you what," said Aunt Opal. "If you both take a bite, then we'll all be in the 'I Ate Something Gross' Club."

"Just one bite and we're in the club?" Stink asked.

Aunt Opal nodded.

"Pass the hot dogs!" said Judy.

Mmm-mmm. They ate up every last bite.

"Yay!" said Stink. "Now we're all in the Gross Grub Club!"

CHAPTER TWO

Stink's Stinky Homework

A week later, Stink was *still* talking about Bigfoot NONSTOP. They were also talking about Bigfoot on the local news. Bigfoot fever was taking over the town!

Stink walked into the kitchen.

"Why are you dressed like a tree?" Judy asked.

"It's my berry-bush disguise. My

Bigfoot club is having an emergency meeting," Stink told Judy. "Wanna come? It starts in fourteen minutes and thirty-seven seconds."

"Bigfoot is for bozos!" said Judy.

"Just don't ask for my autograph when I'm famous for catching him," said Stink.

Bigfoot? BIG DEAL! thought Judy.

While Stink was gone, Judy and Aunt Opal took out Aunt Opal's gigantic trunk of art supplies. They spent the afternoon making super-fancy hats out of garbage-can lids. They cut, glued, pasted, and painted for hours.

"It's mega-cool making such a mess!" said Judy. She was gluing some plastic bugs on her hat when Stink walked in.

"Guess what!" he said. "Zeke, the leader of our Bigfoot club, gave me homework! I have to look for Bigfoot scat."

"Are you sure he wasn't telling *you* to scat?" Judy joked.

"No," said Stink. "*Scat* is another word for doo-doo."

"Doo-doo stop talking about scat," said Judy.

"Scat is POOP!"

"I'm POOPED from all this talk about poop!" Judy said.

Just then they heard the ice-cream truck drive by.

Tingalinga, ding! Ding! Ding!

Stink and Aunt Opal raced for the door.

"Wait for me!" Judy called.

Judy started to run for her piggy bank. Her legs moved, her left hand moved, but her right hand did not.

She pulled, but that hand wouldn't budge.

She pulled harder, but her hand *still* didn't move one single inch. It was glued to the table!

"Help!" she called. "My hand! It's stuck!"

It took exactly one hour and forty-seven minutes to free Judy's hand.

"I had no idea that glue was so strong!" said Aunt Opal.

"This was the Worst. Day. Of. My. Life," said Judy.

"I'm sorry," said Aunt Opal. "I'll make it up to you. Anything you want."

"Really?" Judy asked. "Anything?"

Aunt Opal nodded. "Yes," she said.

Judy knew *exactly* what she wanted. While she was stuck she had seen something in the newspaper on the table—an ad for a midnight zombie walk through the graveyard. Spooky times ten!

"I want to go to this," said Judy, pointing at the paper. "The Creep 'n' Crawl at the cemetery."

"Absolutely!" said Aunt Opal.

Sick-awesome, thought Judy. She couldn't wait.

CHAPTER THREE

At last it was the day of the Creep 'n'
Crawl!

Aunt Opal made sandwiches so they
could have a creeped-out picnic in the
cemetery. She put each sandwich into a
plastic bag when she was done.

Stink was putting something else
into plastic bags—his Bigfoot club
homework: scat!

Finally everyone was ready!

"Let's get to that graveyard," said
Aunt Opal. She grabbed the picnic
basket and started to walk down the
street.

"Where you are you going?" Judy asked. "The cemetery is a zillion miles away. You have to drive."

Aunt Opal looked worried.

"It's okay," Judy said. "You can drive Dad's car."

Aunt Opal looked even more nervous. "Let's ride bikes!" she said.

"We aren't allowed to ride bikes at night," Stink said. "You do know how to drive, right?"

"Of course! I drove across the Horn of Africa," she said. They all climbed into the car. "Ten years ago," she added.

Aunt Opal stepped on the gas.

Vrrooom!

She almost hit the garage door.

"WATCH OUT!" Judy and Stink hollered.

Aunt Opal slammed on the brakes. *Screech!*

Then she stepped on the gas again, and they flew out of the driveway.

"You call this driving?" Stink asked.

"It'll come back to me," said Aunt Opal as they zoomed forward.

"SLOW DOWN!" Judy and Stink cried.

They sped and swerved around the neighborhood.

"Do you know how to get there?" Aunt Opal asked. "I have no idea where I'm going!"

Judy searched around for map. She finally found one on the floor. She picked it up just as they *flew* over a bump.

Ba-dump!

The map *flew* out the window.

Aunt Opal kept driving—or trying to. It seemed like they had been in the car FOREVER. As they drove past an old

amusement park for third time, the car
made a not-good noise.

Splutter, splutter, splunk.

"Uh-oh," said Aunt Opal. "We're out
of gas."

"Not to mention Way. Super. Lost,"
said Stink.

CHAPTER FOUR

The Poop Picnic

"Can we eat?" asked Stink. "I'm starving."

Aunt Opal found an old teacup ride, and they all sat down inside one of the giant teacups.

"Look at that!" Aunt Opal said, trying to smile. She pointed to a sign behind them. "We're eating in the Fun Zone."

The *F* was missing from the words FUN ZONE.

"You mean the UN-Zone," said Judy.

"It's not *that* bad," said Aunt Opal. She handed out the sandwiches.

Judy was super bummed that they hadn't made it to the cemetery. But she was Bigfoot-hungry. So she sat down and pulled out her sandwich.

She didn't see the lump stuck to the bread.

It was brown.

It was . . . stinky.

Stink sniffed his sandwich.

"Mine smells funny," he said. "Almost like . . ."

Judy raised her sandwich.

She opened her mouth.

She began to bite down. . . .

Suddenly Stink dropped his sandwich. He grabbed Judy's out of her hands and flipped it over.

They all stared at the brown smelly lump.

"What IS that?" asked Judy.

"It's scat!" Stink hollered. "Doo-doo. Dung. POOP!"

Stink's sandwich had brown goo on it, too. Grody, grody, GROSS!

"AGGGGGGGGGHHHHHHHHHHHH!"
they shouted.

Aunt Opal slammed the picnic
basket shut.

"I think this picnic is over," said
Aunt Opal. "Let's call a tow truck so we
can get out of here. But what will we do
about dinner?"

"Extra-cheese pizza!" Stink shouted.

"And hold the poop," Judy added.

When everyone finally got home at the end of the summer, they had a poop-free party to celebrate. Judy's friend Rocky showed off some magic tricks. He even sawed her in half!

It was *grrr-8* to have everyone back, but that meant Aunt Opal would be going home, too.

After the party, it was time for Aunt Opal to say good-bye. "How about you just don't leave and stay with us? We can have pizza every night!" Judy said.

"I have to go," said Aunt Opal, "but I'm going to miss you lots! And I'm glad your summer wasn't a *total* bummer, after all."

"Me, too!" said Judy. "I had the best summer ever—with you! After all, how many people can say they've been on a poop picnic?"